For my brother, Christopher, and for Molly Bang,
whose work inspired me to become an illustrator.

Library of Congress Cataloging-in-Publication Data is available.

ISBN 978-1-4521-6100-6

Manufactured in China.

MIX
Paper from
responsible sources
FSC™ C008047

Design by Jennifer Tolo Pierce.
Typeset in Agenda.
The illustrations in this book were rendered in graphite,
pen and ink, watercolor, and colored pencil.

10 9 8 7 6 5 4 3 2

Chronicle books and gifts are available at special quantity
discounts to corporations, professional associations, literacy
programs, and other organizations. For details and discount
information, please contact our premiums department at
corporatesales@chroniclebooks.com or at 1-800-759-0190.

Chronicle Books LLC
680 Second Street
San Francisco, California 94107

Chronicle Books—we see things differently. Become part
of our community at www.chroniclekids.com.

BRAVE MOLLY

Brooke Boynton-Hughes

chronicle books · san francisco

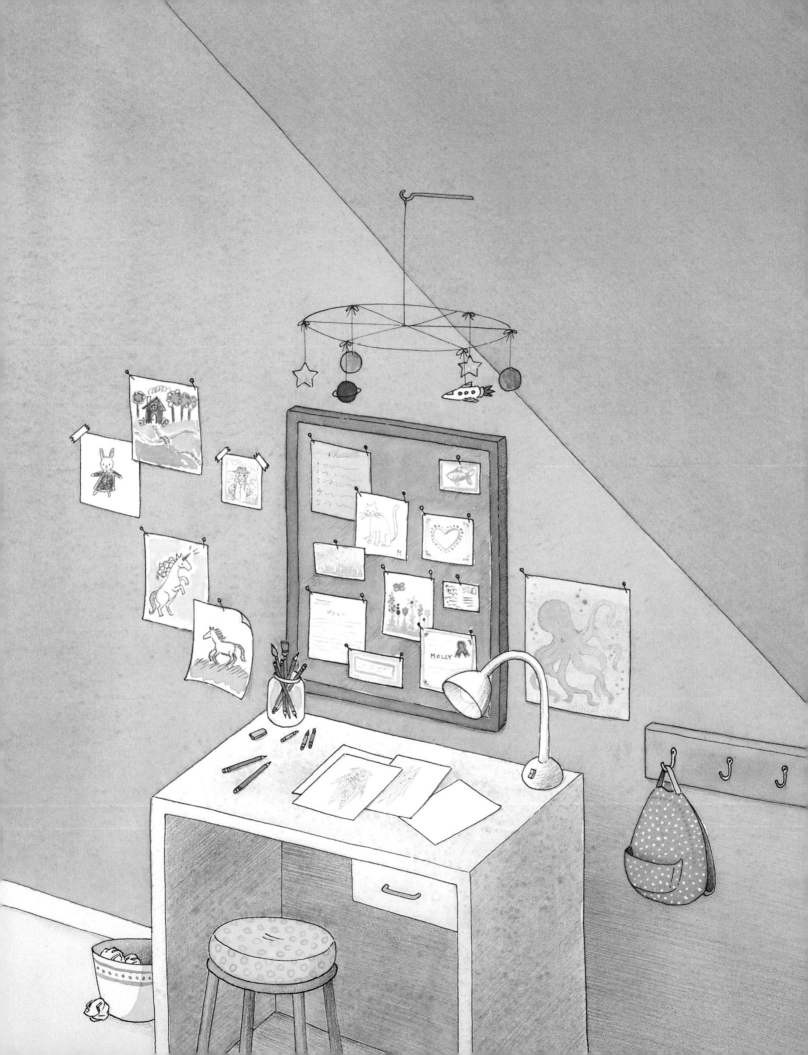